Copyright © 2022 by Dr. Lori M. Philips
All rights reserved. This book or any portion thereof
may not be reproduced or used in any manner whatsoever
without the express written permission of the publisher
except for the use of brief quotations in a book review.

Lizzie
and the Weird Kid in Apartment 2B

Written by:
Dr. Lori M. Phillips

Illustrated by:
Prosenjit Roy

One hot sunny morning, as Timothy prepared for school, he splashed a few sprinkles of water on his face, sang a little of the alphabet song to make sure that he'd brushed his teeth long enough, pulled his shirt over his head, spat on his hands and ran them through his tightly twisted locs.

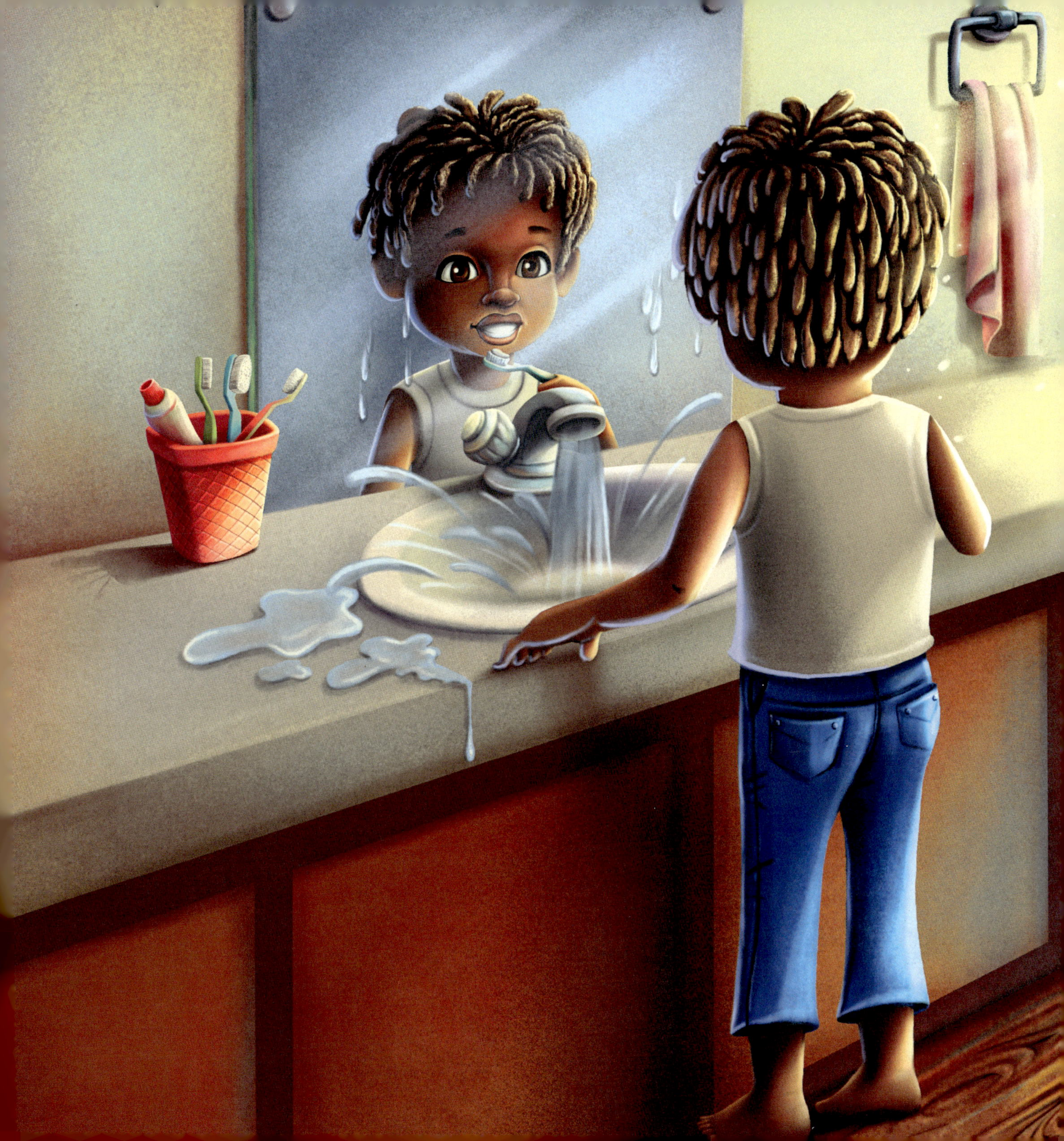

As Timothy walked towards the door, he yelled, " I love you! See you when I get back home."

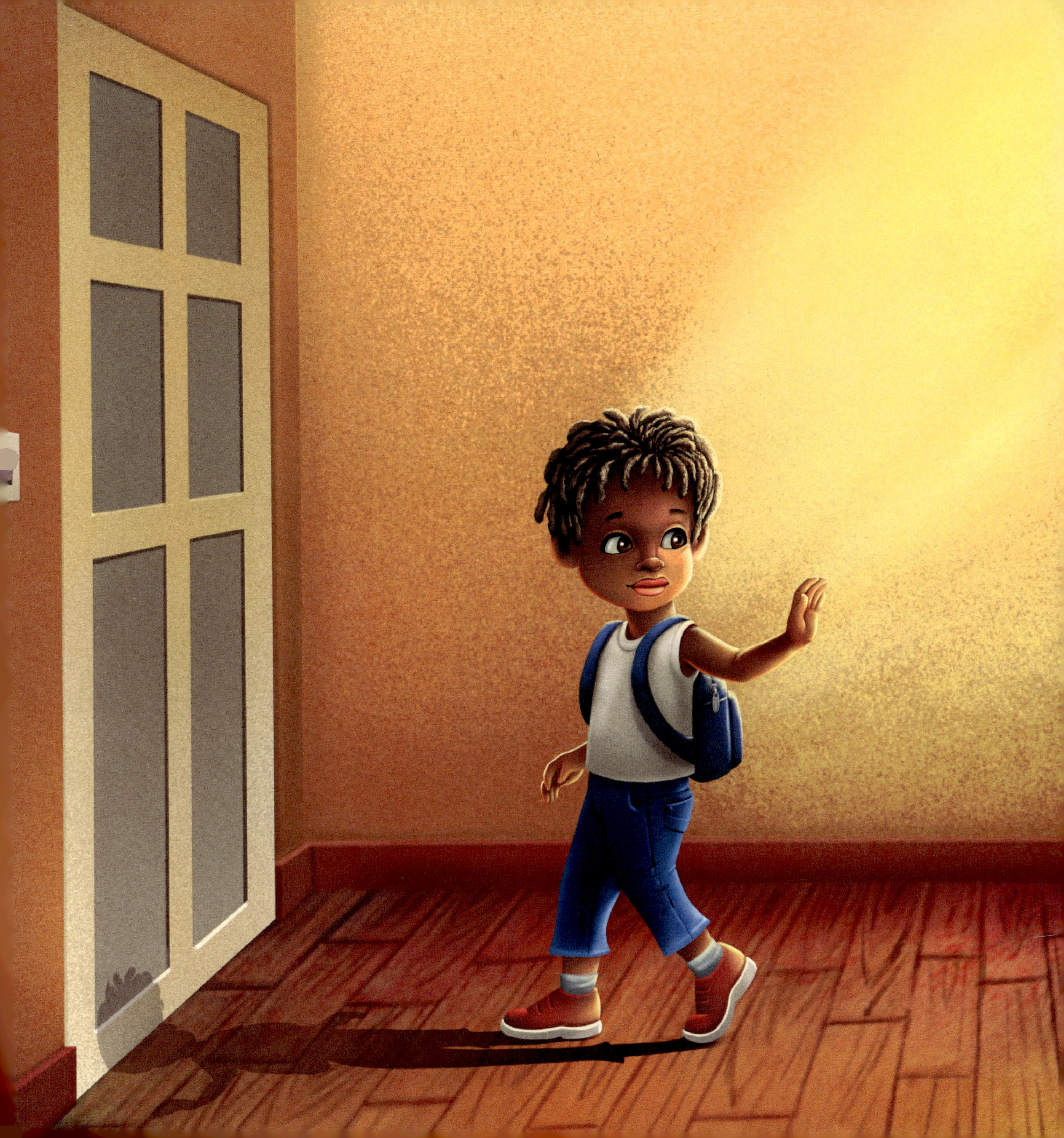

Timothy walked outside and saw a group of kids walking past his apartment building heading to school. He quickly dashed to hide behind the column in front of his apartment door and waited on the group to pass him by while gripping the column for dear life!

As he continued to hide behind the column, Lizzie, one of the kids in the group, felt her earring fall from her ear and turned around to search for it on the extremely cracked sidewalk.

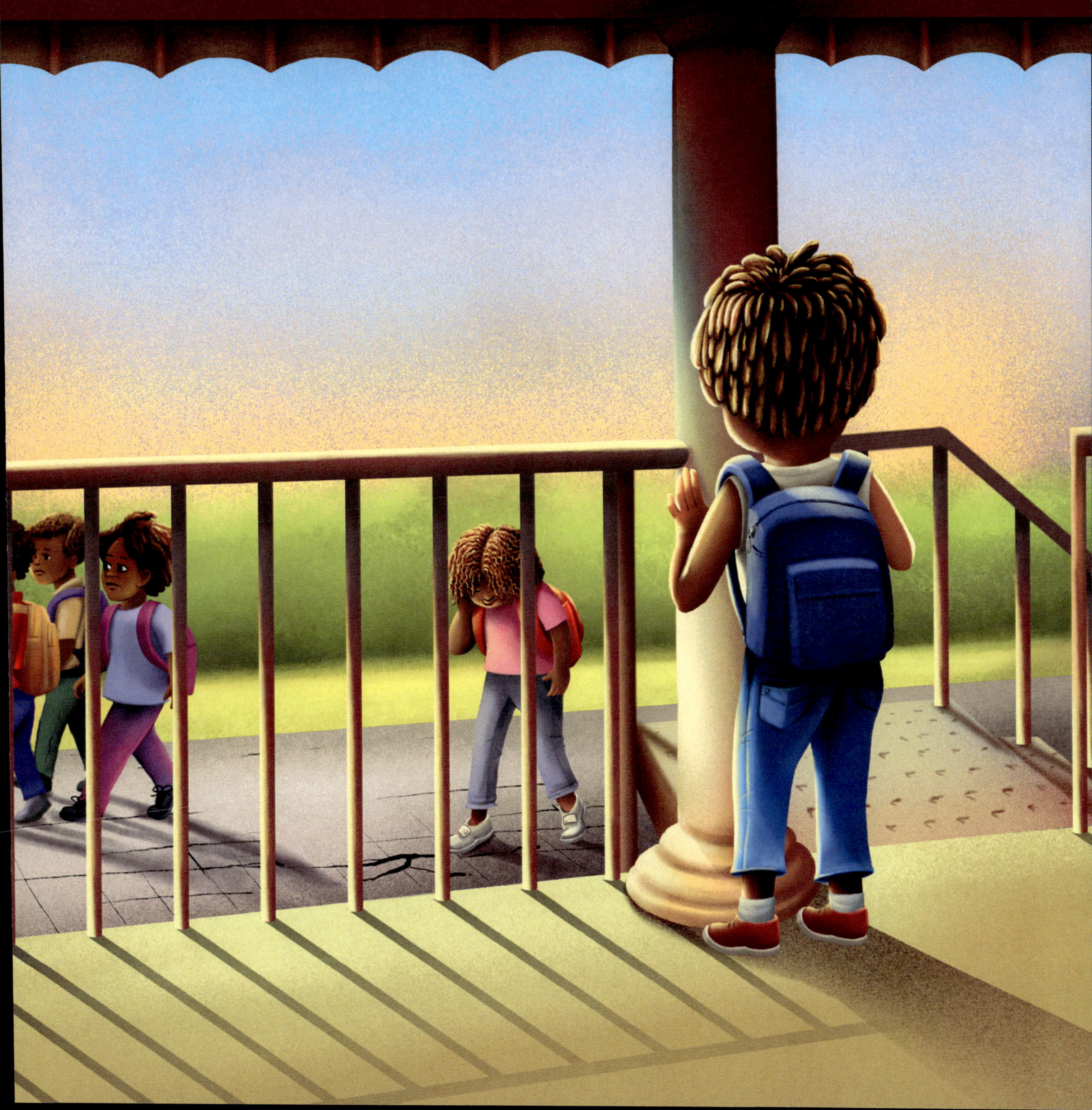

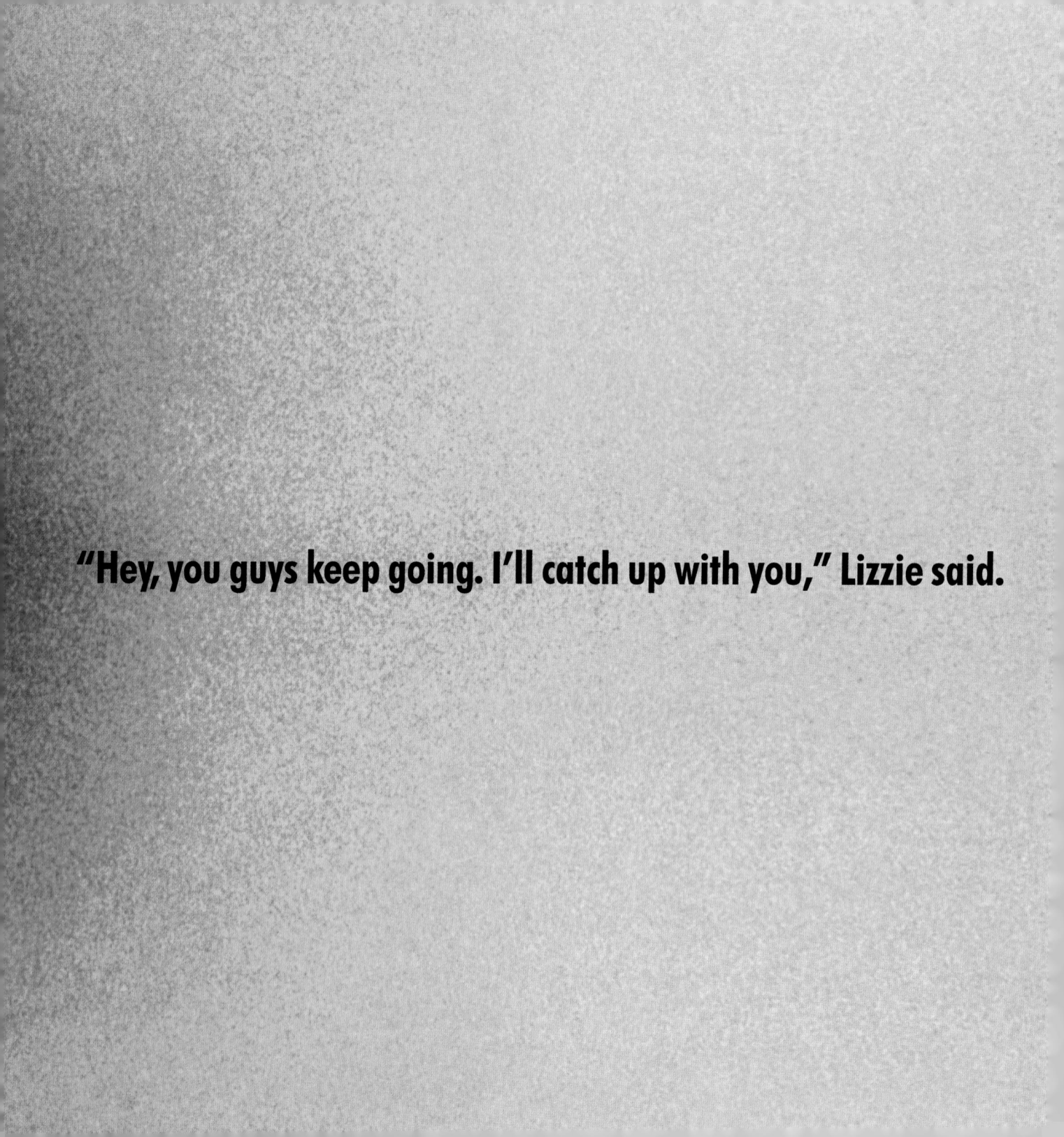

"Hey, you guys keep going. I'll catch up with you," Lizzie said.

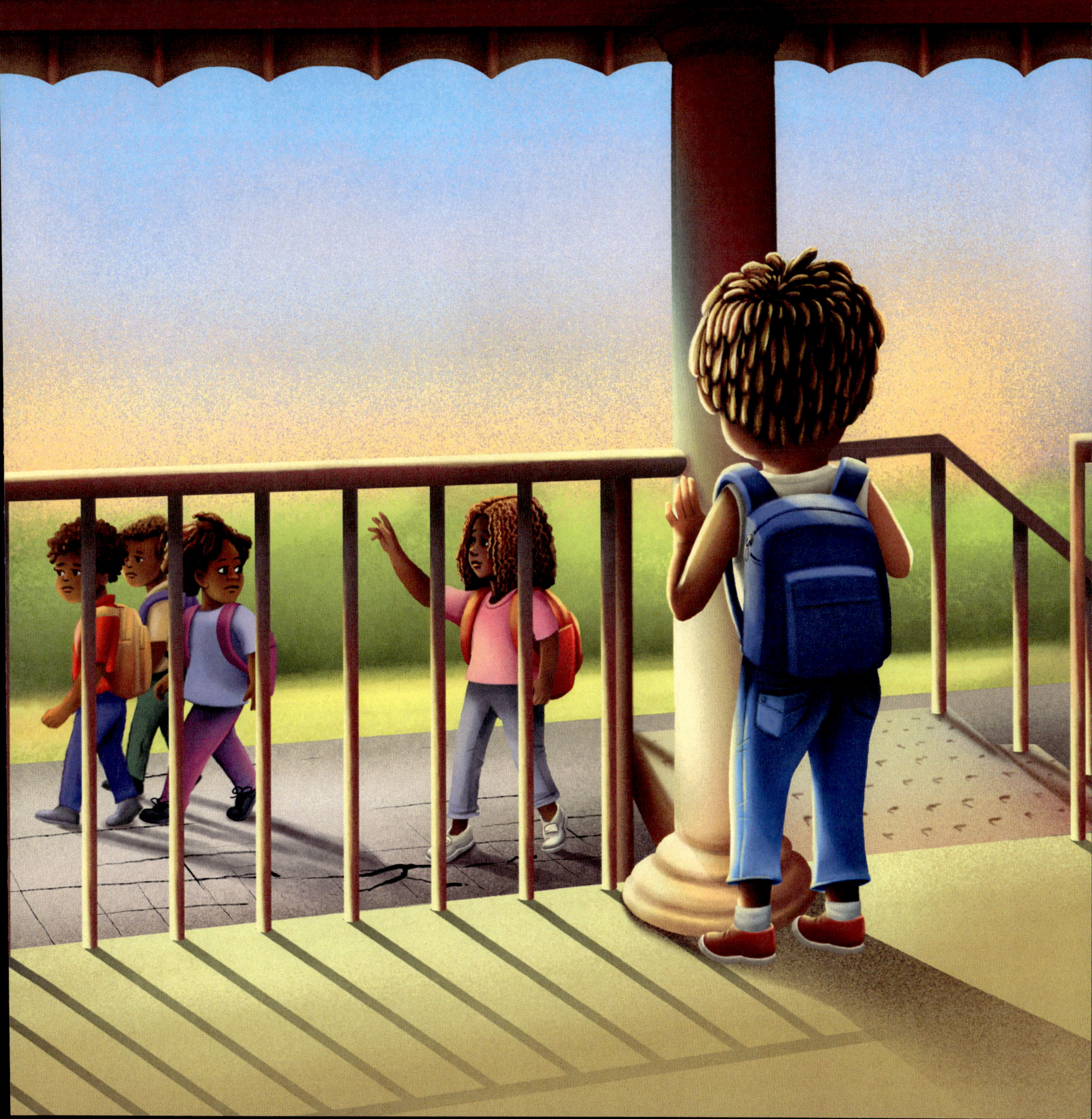

After walking around the area where she felt the earring fall, she spotted the tassel of her earring peeping through a z-shaped crack in the middle of the sidewalk. "Whew, that was close; glad I found it!" As Lizzie raised slowly and still smiling, her eyes locked instantly with Timothy's eyes.

 He was standing stiffly beside the column. Lizzie appeared startled.

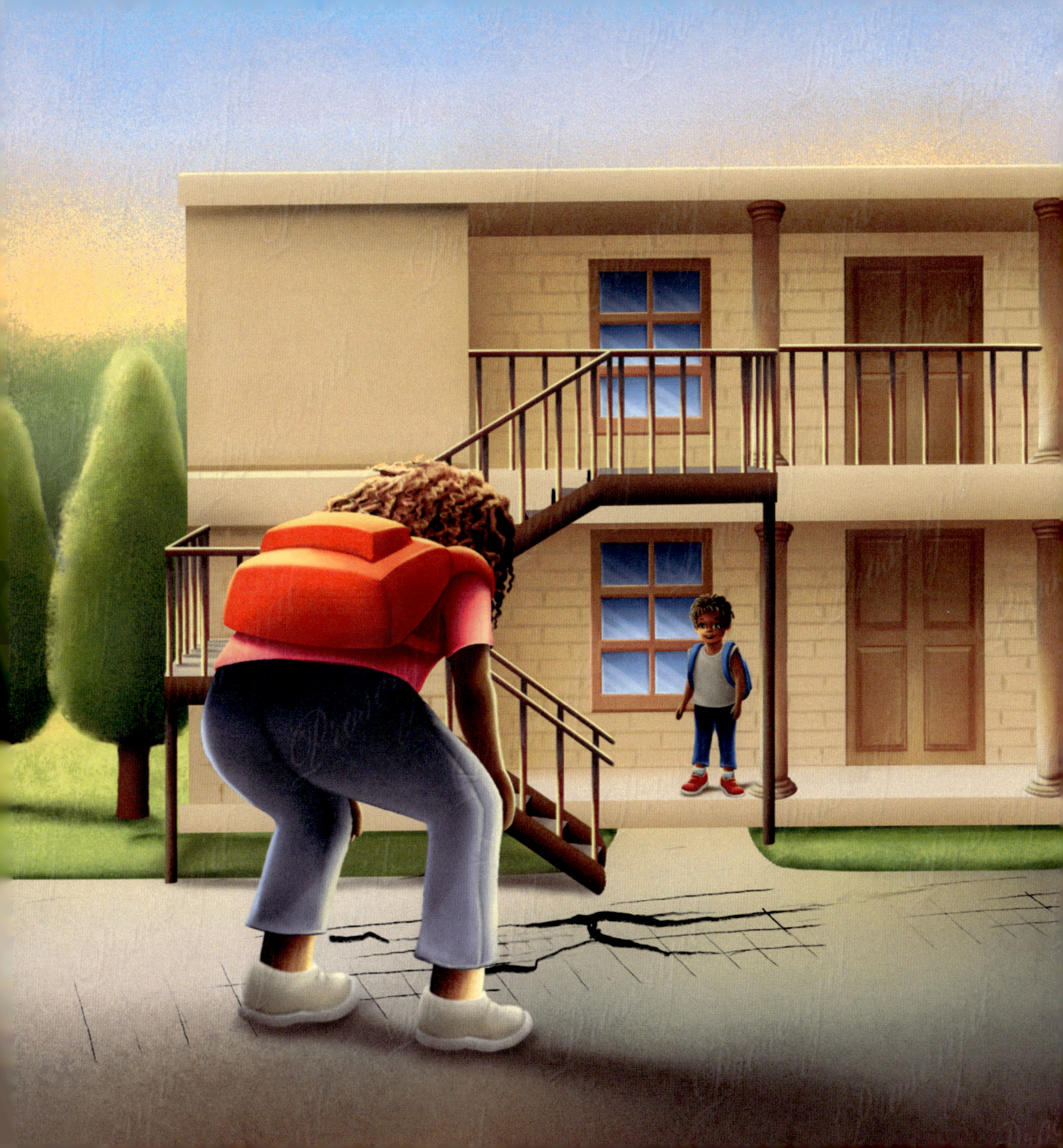

As she caught up with friends and shared how she saw this weird guy staring at her. Timothy was so ashamed. "Oh, no!" He whispered embarrassingly. "That was THE LAST thing I needed this morning!" Lizzie and her friends faded out of sight, Timothy, alone, proceeded in a slow walk to school.

Lizzie never noticed before, but Timothy, known to her as the weird kid, was actually in her class and sat right behind her. Yes, he was just that quiet. It was like he was not there. The teacher never called on him, and no one talked to him. While he was not at all a bad child, Timothy just seemed weird, at least according to Lizzie. Each time she would turn around to try to get a stare long enough to figure him out, he'd be staring back at her.

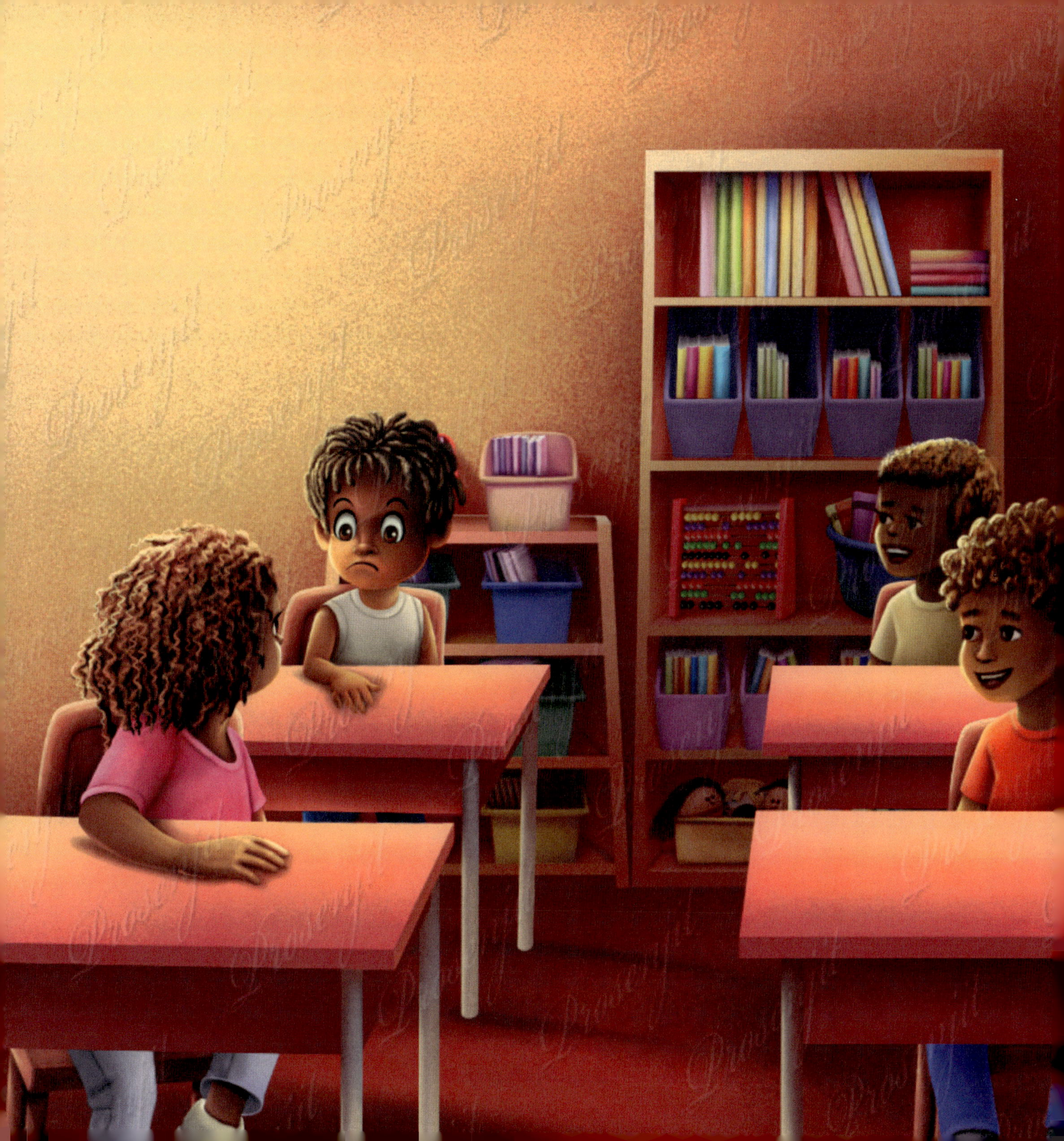

On the way home, as Lizzie and her same group of friends were walking from school, Timothy ran swiftly past them, clearly in a rush. "Hey, that's the guy that I was telling you about this morning." Josh, one of Lizzie's friends, asked, "You mean the weirdo?" The group laughed. "Yes, that was him that just ran past us." They all began to shout, "Hey, Weirdo, slow down!" "Hey, Weirdo, do you hear us talking to you?" Timothy stopped, turned around angrily with his chest protruding from the hard run, took a hard look at Lizzie, and continued running.

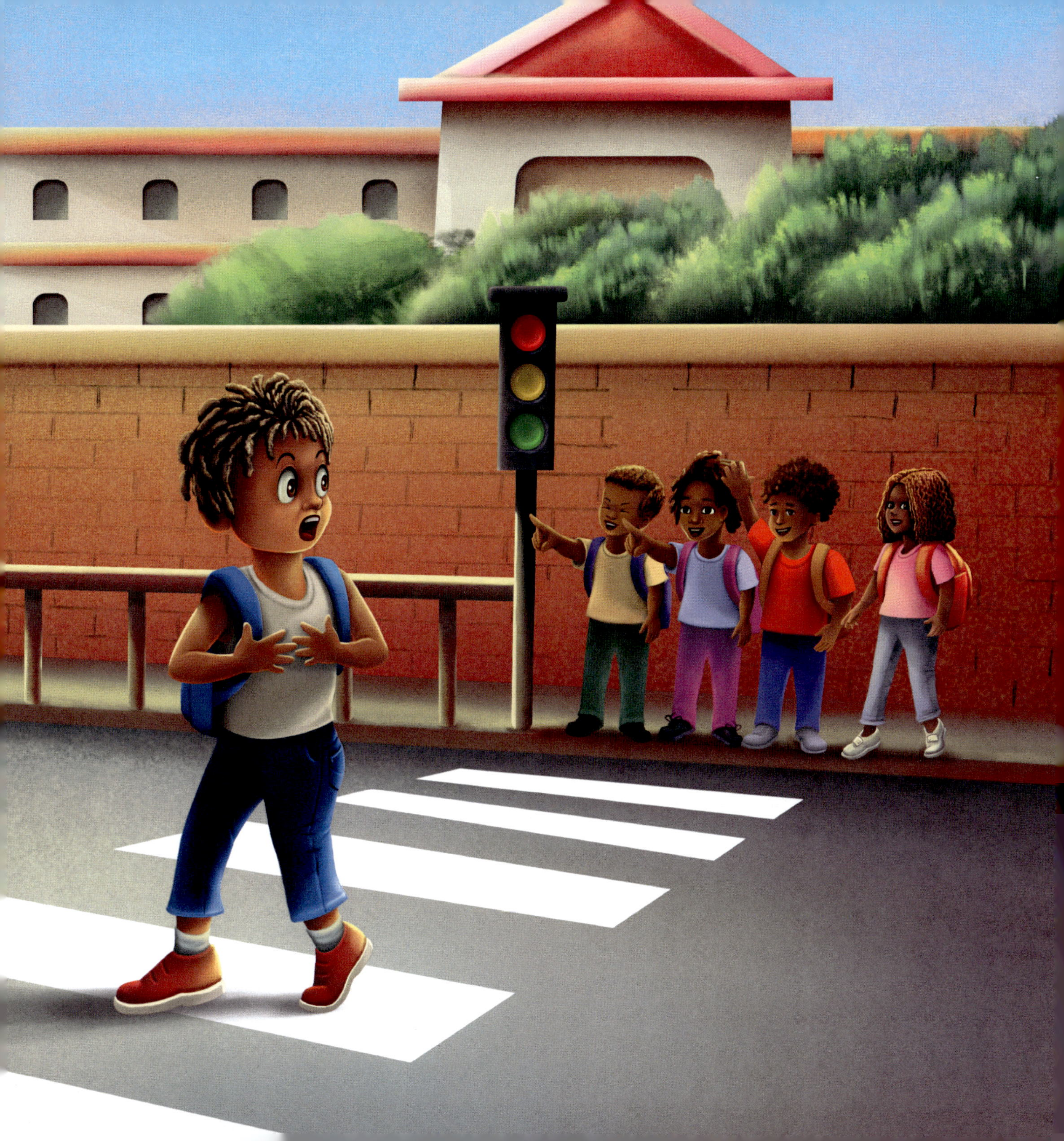

As they passed his apartment window, they noticed someone peeping through the blinds, but they couldn't make out who it was. It appeared that it was someone wearing a dark-colored mask. The blind would open, then close, open, then close, open, then quickly close.

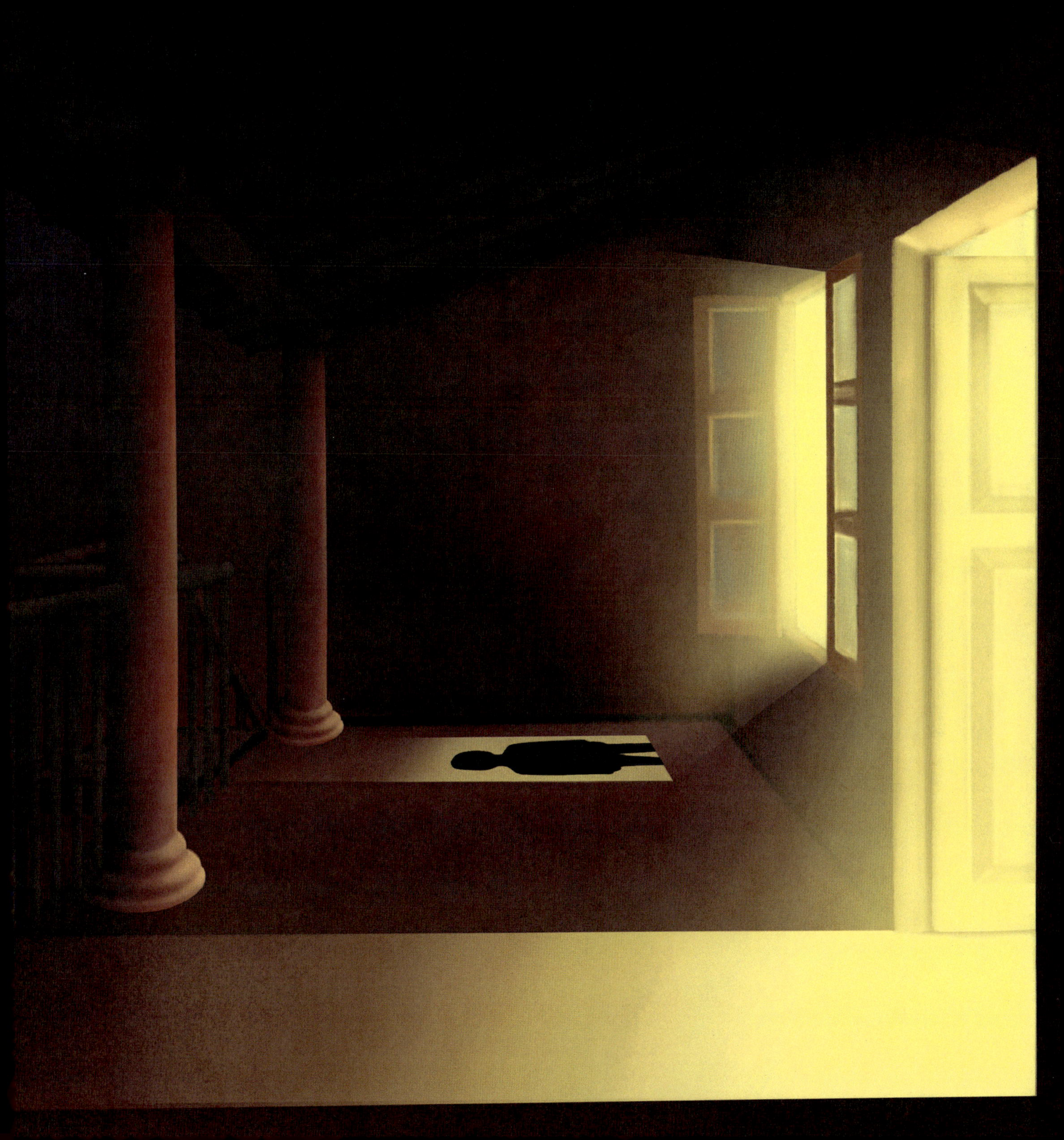

"Hey, I have a cool idea," said Lizzie. "Let's meet up tonight to find out more about this guy." She was just that curious! " Yeah, let's go to his apartment and scare the guy into talking!"

As night fell, the group of friends met on the side of Apartment 2B. Slowly peeping around the complex, Lizzie's crew looked up and saw the person with the black mask opening the blinds and shining a blinding bright light in their direction. They all quickly ducked.

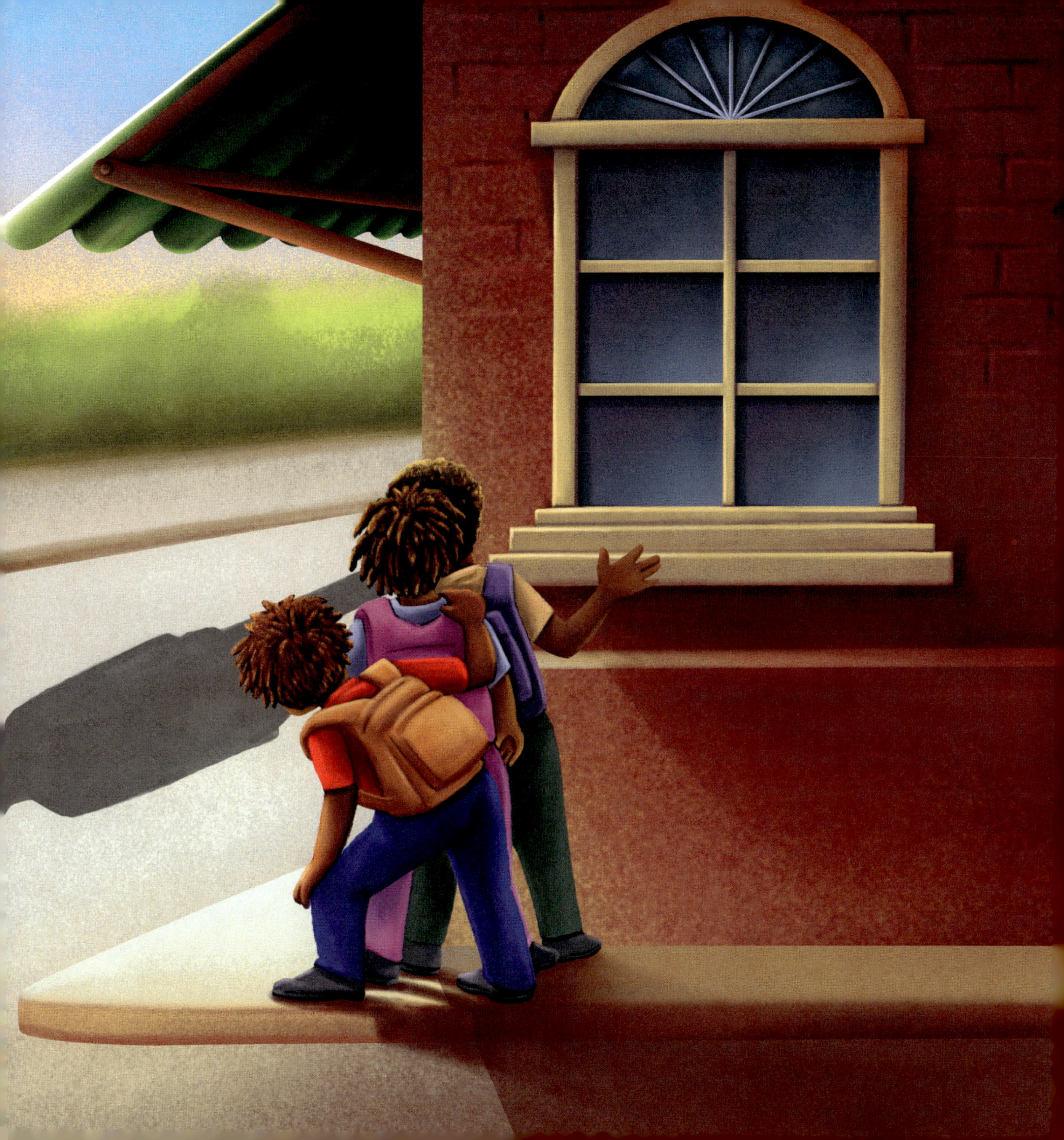

As they tiptoed up the stairs, they saw a larger shadow pulling something OR someone into what appeared to be a closet (it may have been their imagination playing tricks on them). "Oh, no! What if the weirdo is a kid-napper!" whispered someone in the group. "What if he's a parent-napper?" whispered another person in the group. They had three steps remaining before making it to the top of the stairs where Timothy's apartment was. The large frame appeared again and could be seen pushing another person. By this time, the group was frightened but also even more curious.

Lizzie yelled, "I can't take it! Go back down stairs! I'm going up to the window. I want to see." "Just get ready to run!" Lizzie shouted as she didn't know what was about to happen. As Lizzie walked up to the window, searching for a peephole to look inside, the bright light landed directly on her.

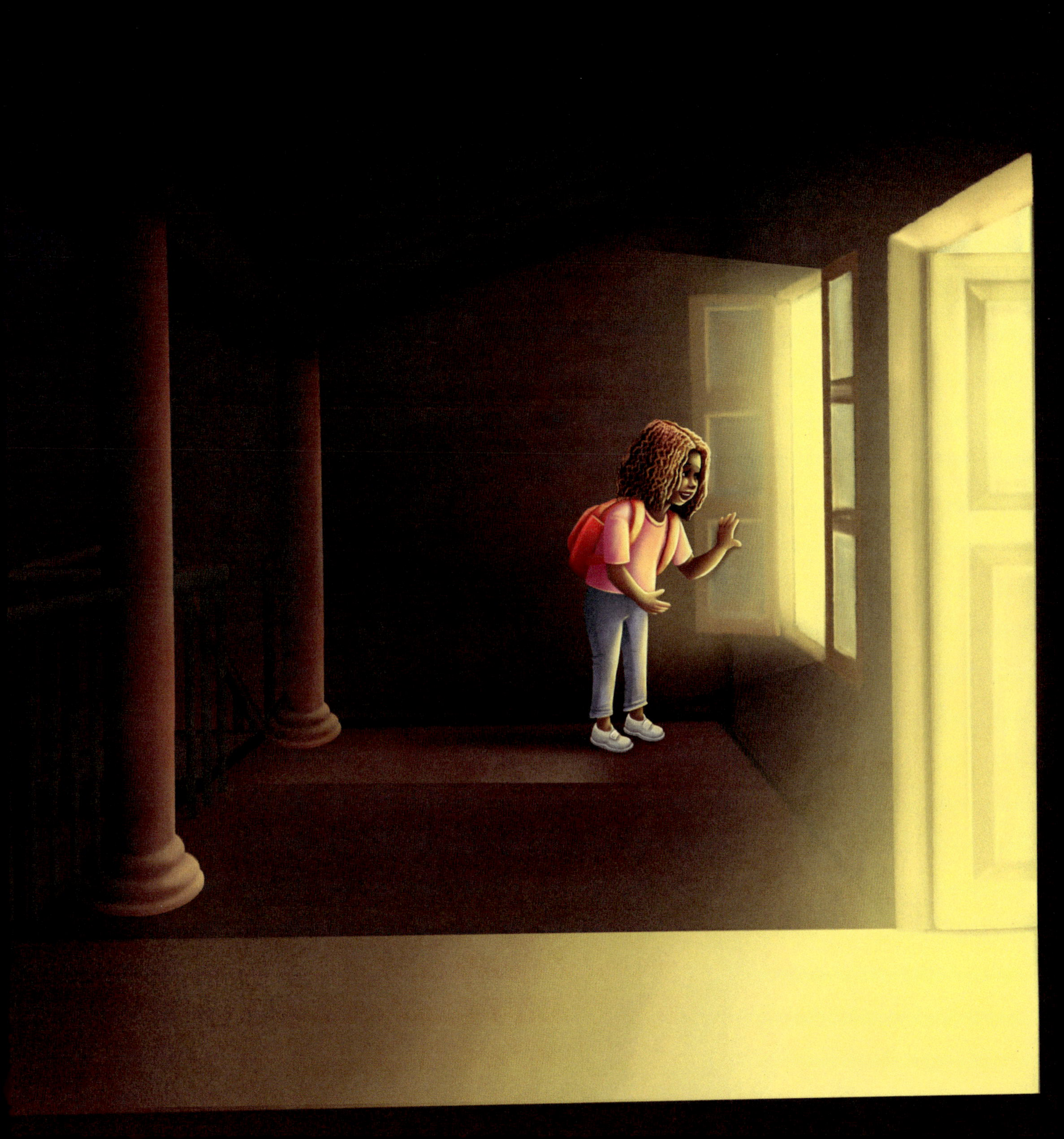

Suddenly, a screeching sound could be heard as the front door slowly opened. Standing was a little boy wearing a black costume and holding a toy race car with bright lights shining on the front. "Hey, wanna play?" asked the little boy innocently. A large shadow appeared. It was Timothy! "What do you want? Why are you at my house?" He asked Lizzie angrily.

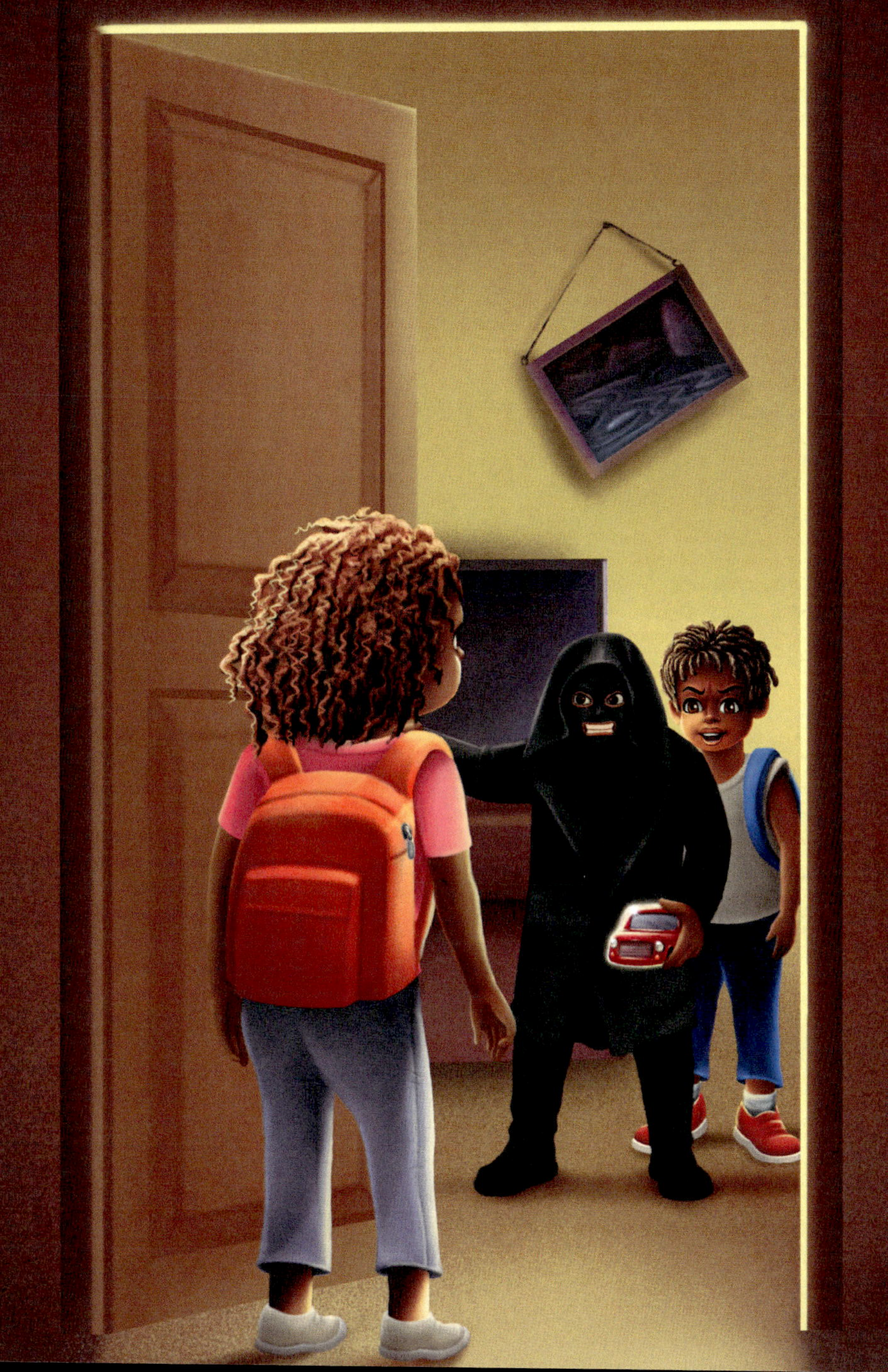

Timothy then turned to the little boy, staring into his mask, and in a gentle tone, said, "Tyler, I'm the big brother. I'm in charge of you. Don't ever open the door without my permission." Tyler looked up at Timothy and gave a simple nod of understanding.

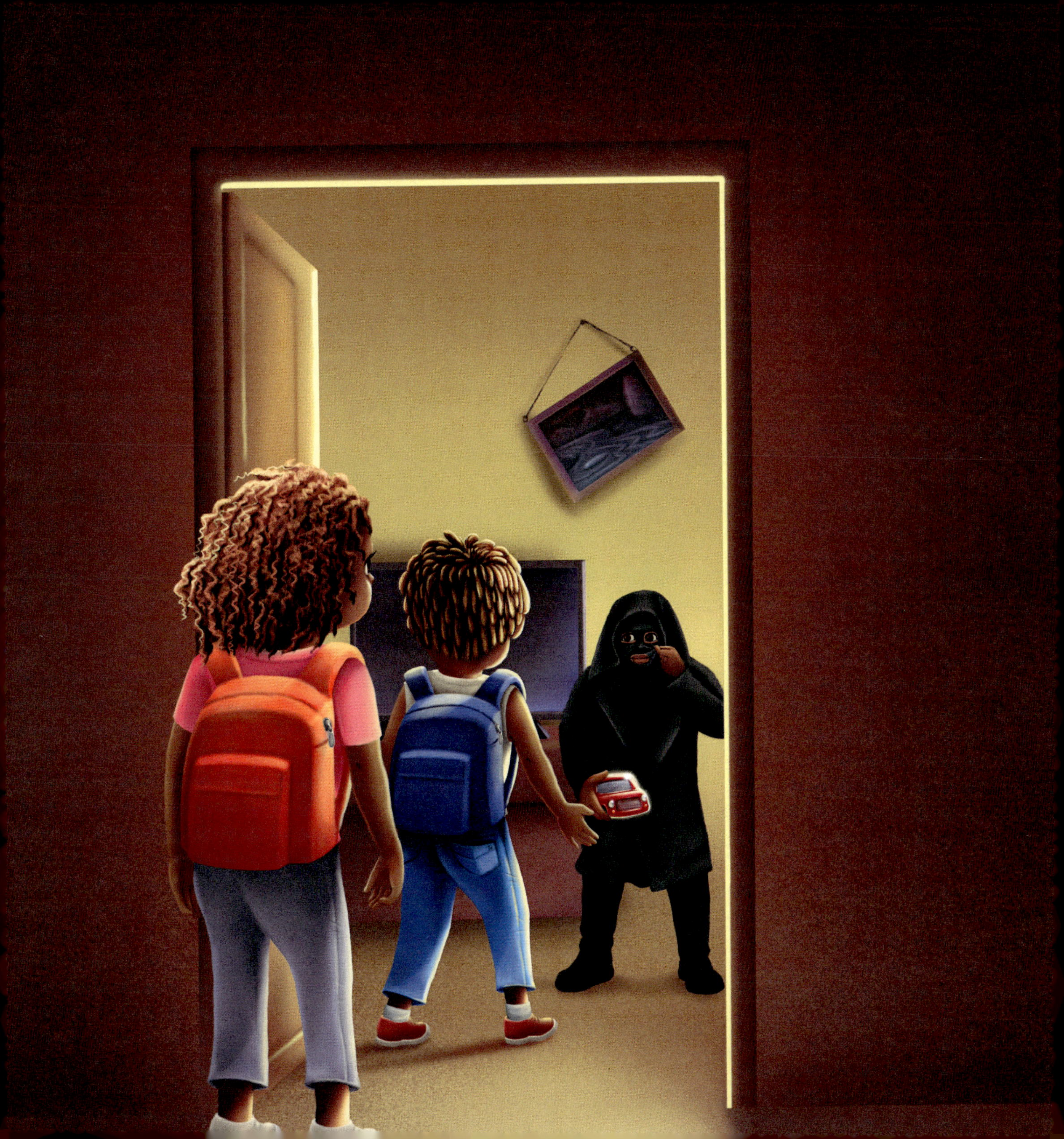

Suddenly, entering the front room and heading towards the door in a wheelchair was an older woman with two long plaits that hung over the backing of the wheelchair. "Tim, I didn't know you had a friend. Let her in," she said. "No, Grandma, she is not my friend, and she is leaving now."

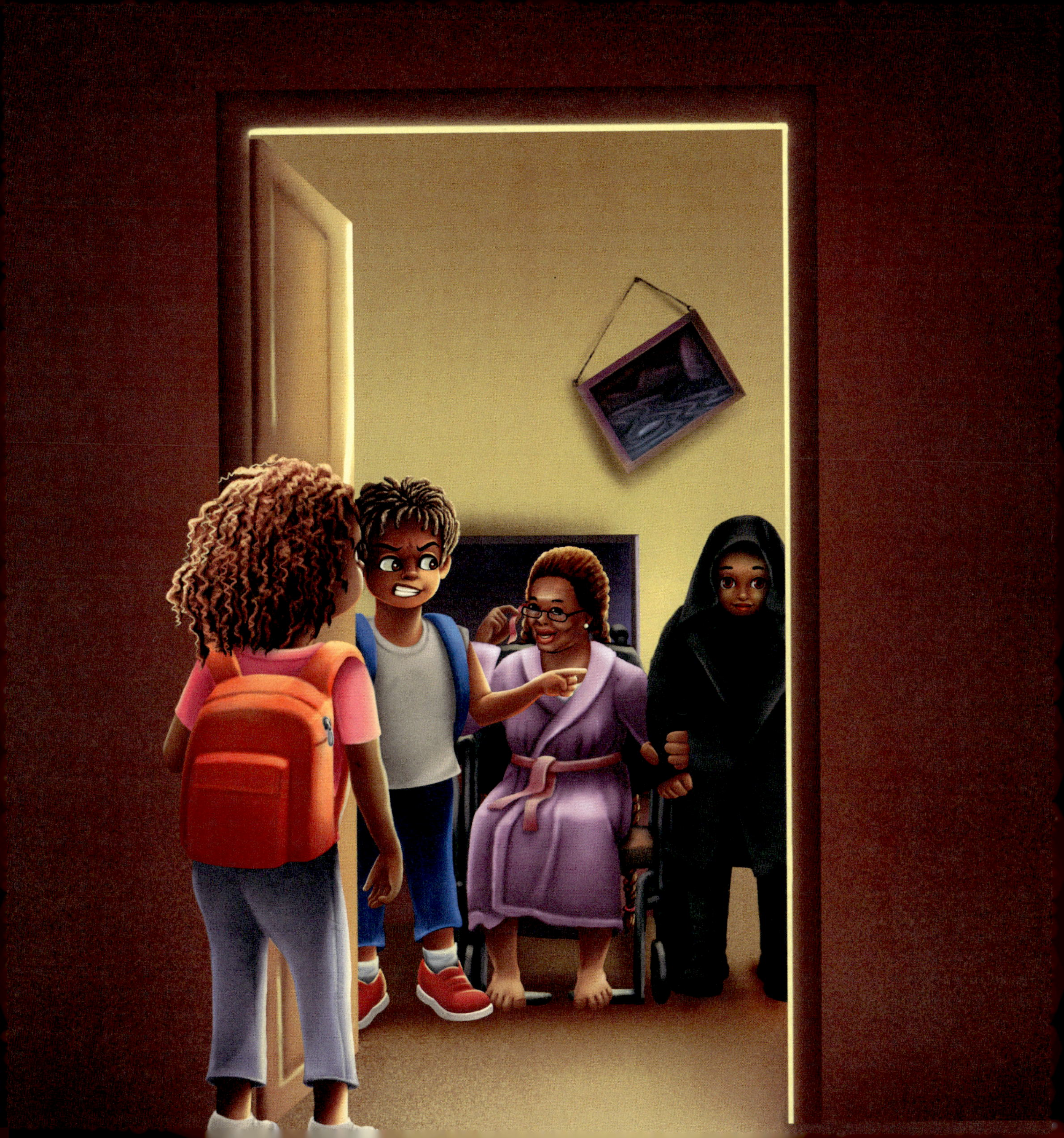

Lizzie felt awful. It turns out Timothy wasn't a weirdo. As she continued to stand outside of the apartment, Lizzie could do nothing but stare into the window.

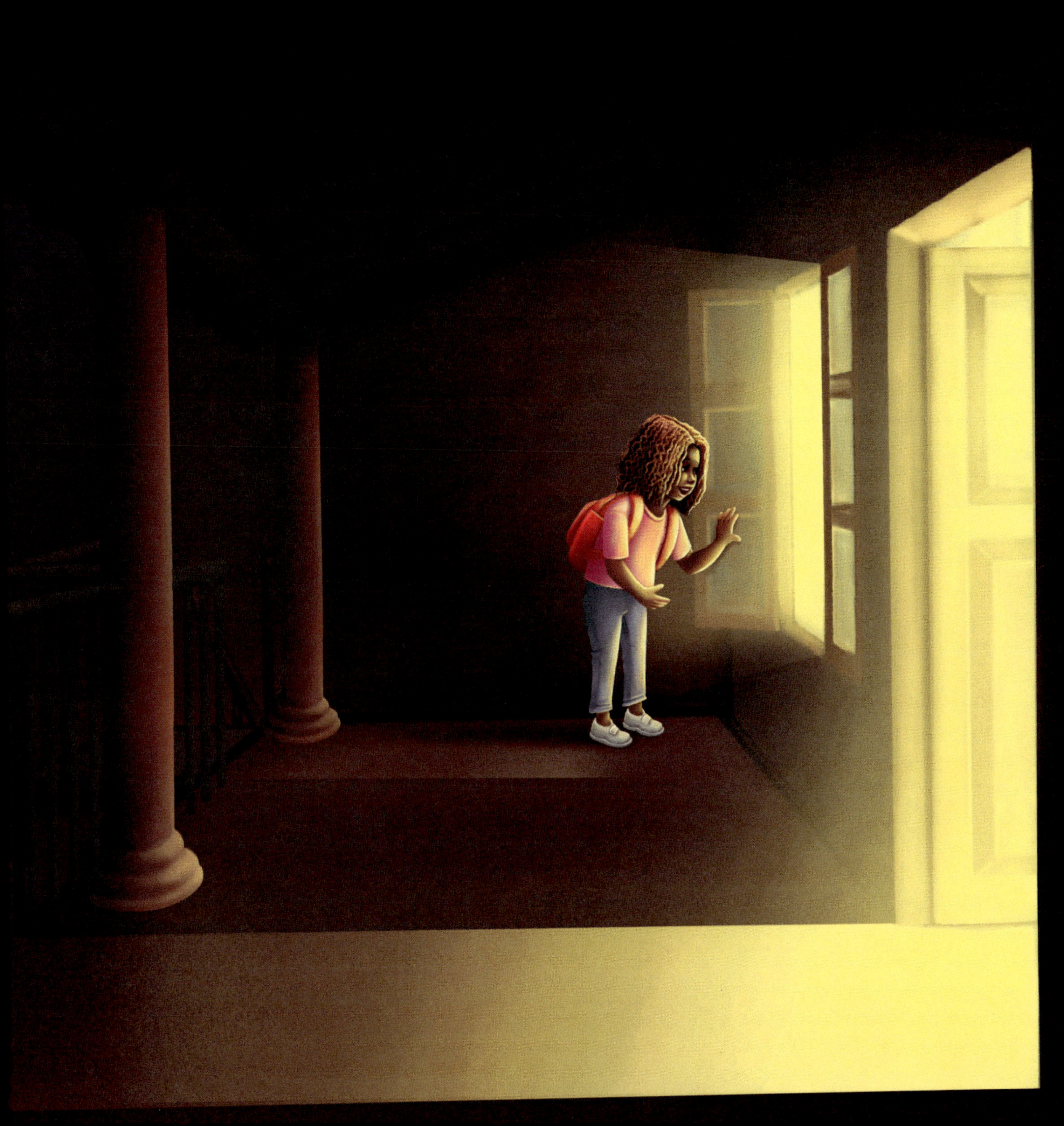

She could see Timothy pushing the grandmother in her wheelchair into the kitchen and placing a napkin around his little brother's neck, preparing for dinner. Timothy was seen wiping food from around his grandmother's mouth and feeding her. Lizzie could do nothing but cry as it was the sweetest gesture she had seen.

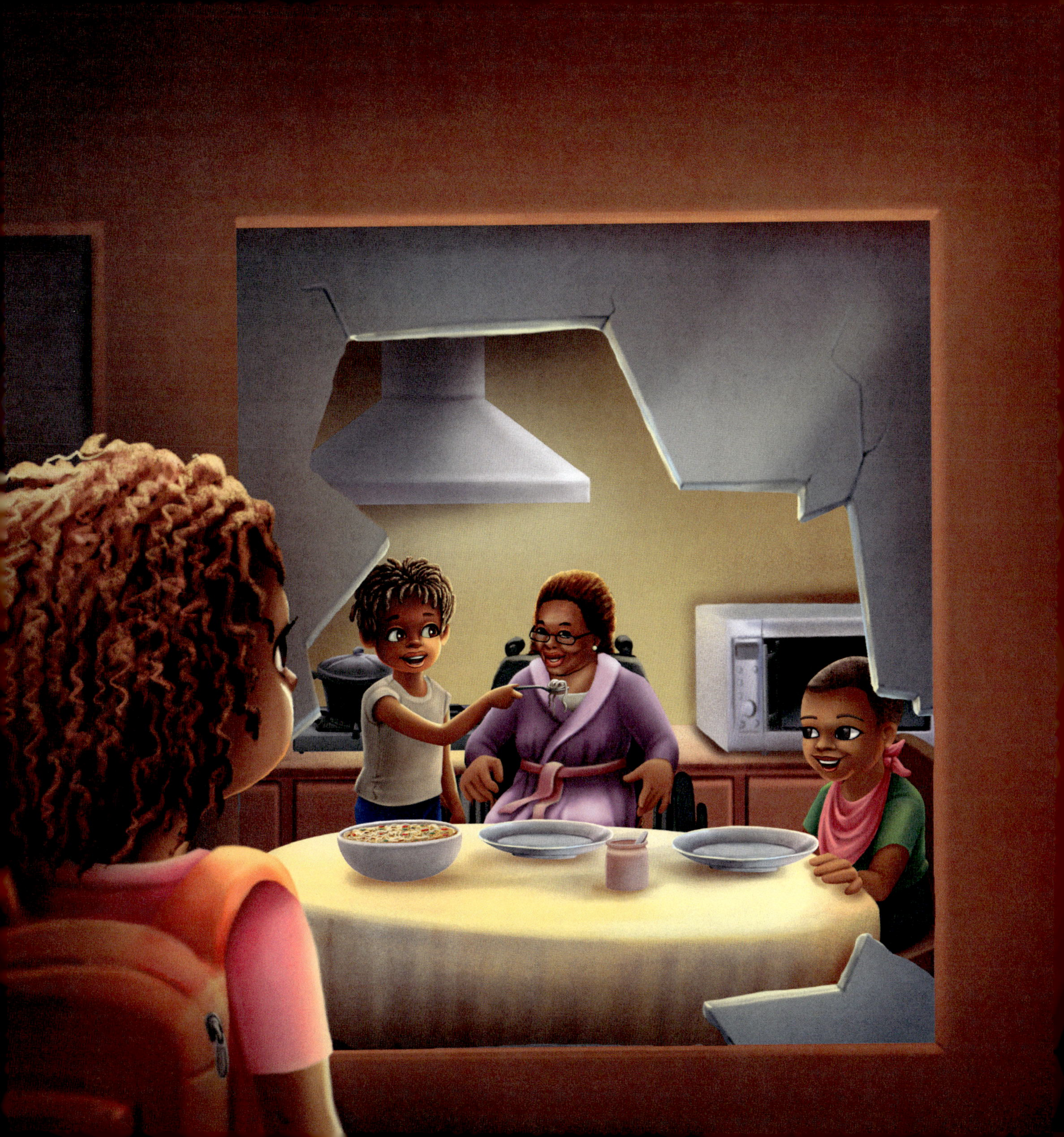

As she slowly walked down the stairs, she could not help but sympathize with Timothy. It all made sense. That is why he was so withdrawn! He had so much responsibility at home that he struggled with actually just being a kid. He had to always act as the adult as his mom worked three jobs. You see, Lizzie discovered that Timothy promised to help his mom because he didn't want to see his grandmother go to a nursing home and she could not afford daycare.

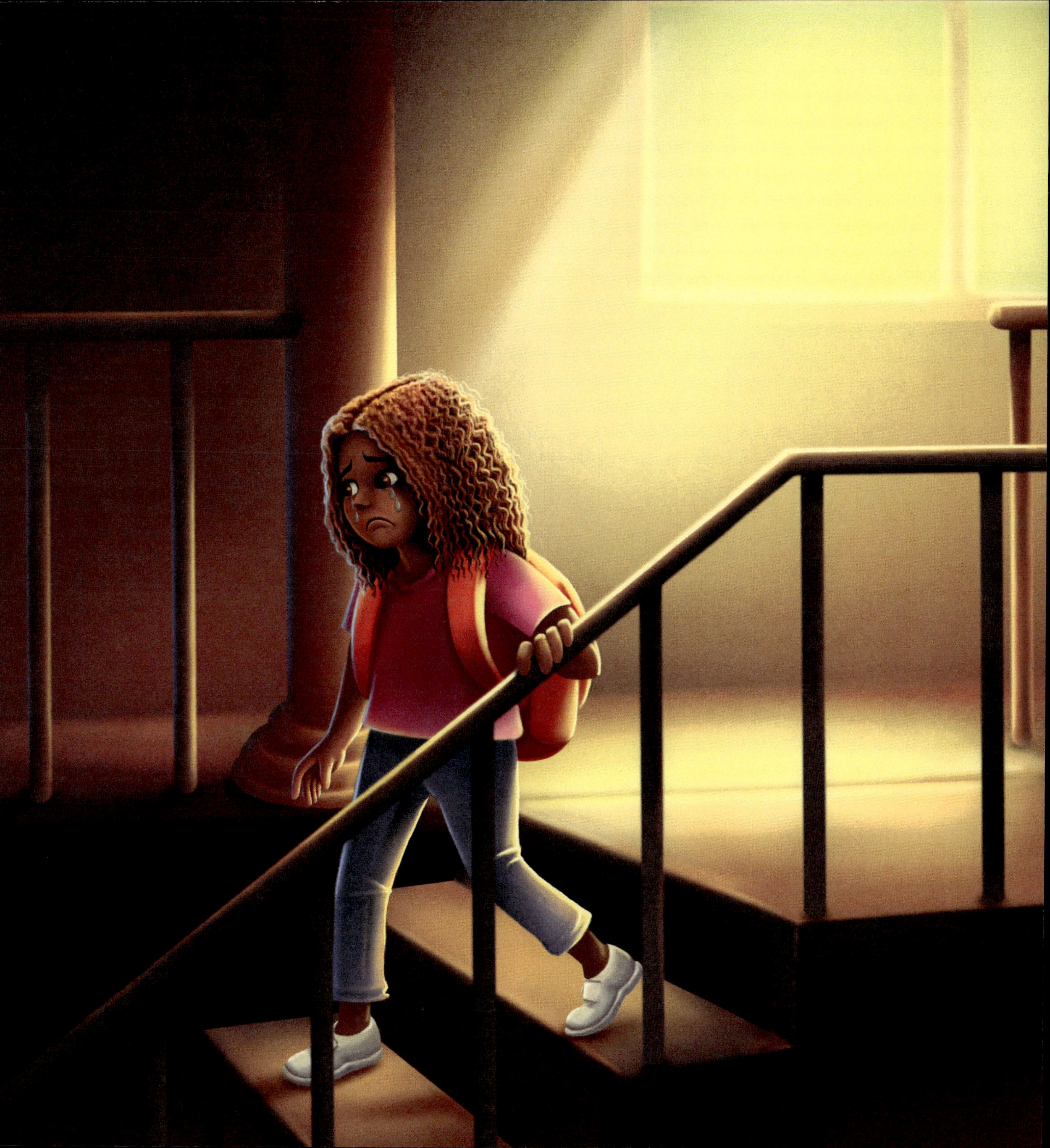

The next morning in class, the teacher shared they would be writing a persuasive essay, but she was trying to think of a topic. Lizzie raised her hand. As the teacher acknowledged her, she looked at Timothy, locking eyes as they always seemed to do, and said, "I have one. I think a perfect topic would be, Should You Judge a Book by Its Cover?".

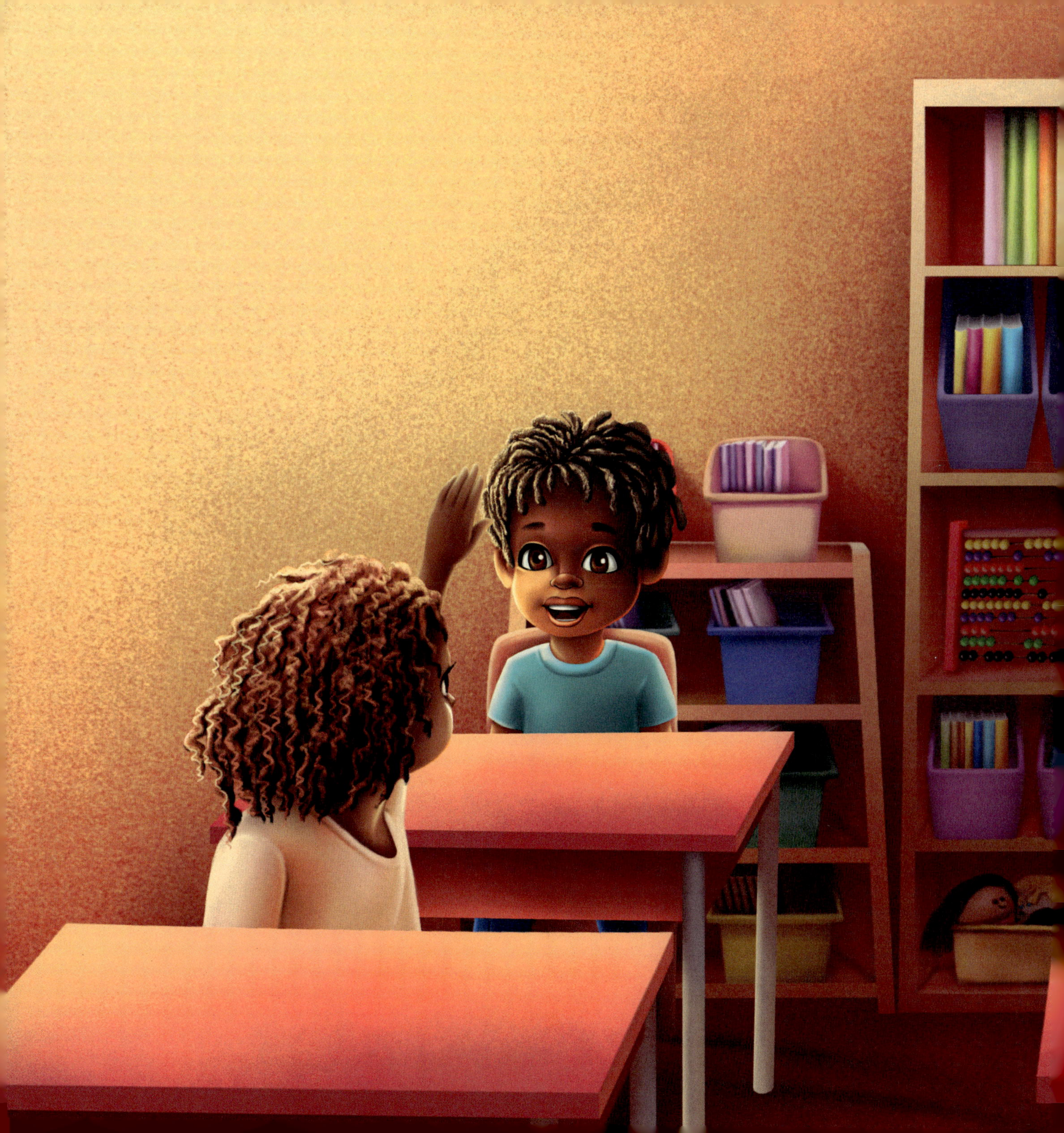

"Why, that's a great topic, Lizzie!" the teacher exclaimed. Lizzie and Timothy both smiled as Lizzie said, "It sure is, and I can't wait to write all about it."

Timothy and Lizzie ended up becoming the best of friends.

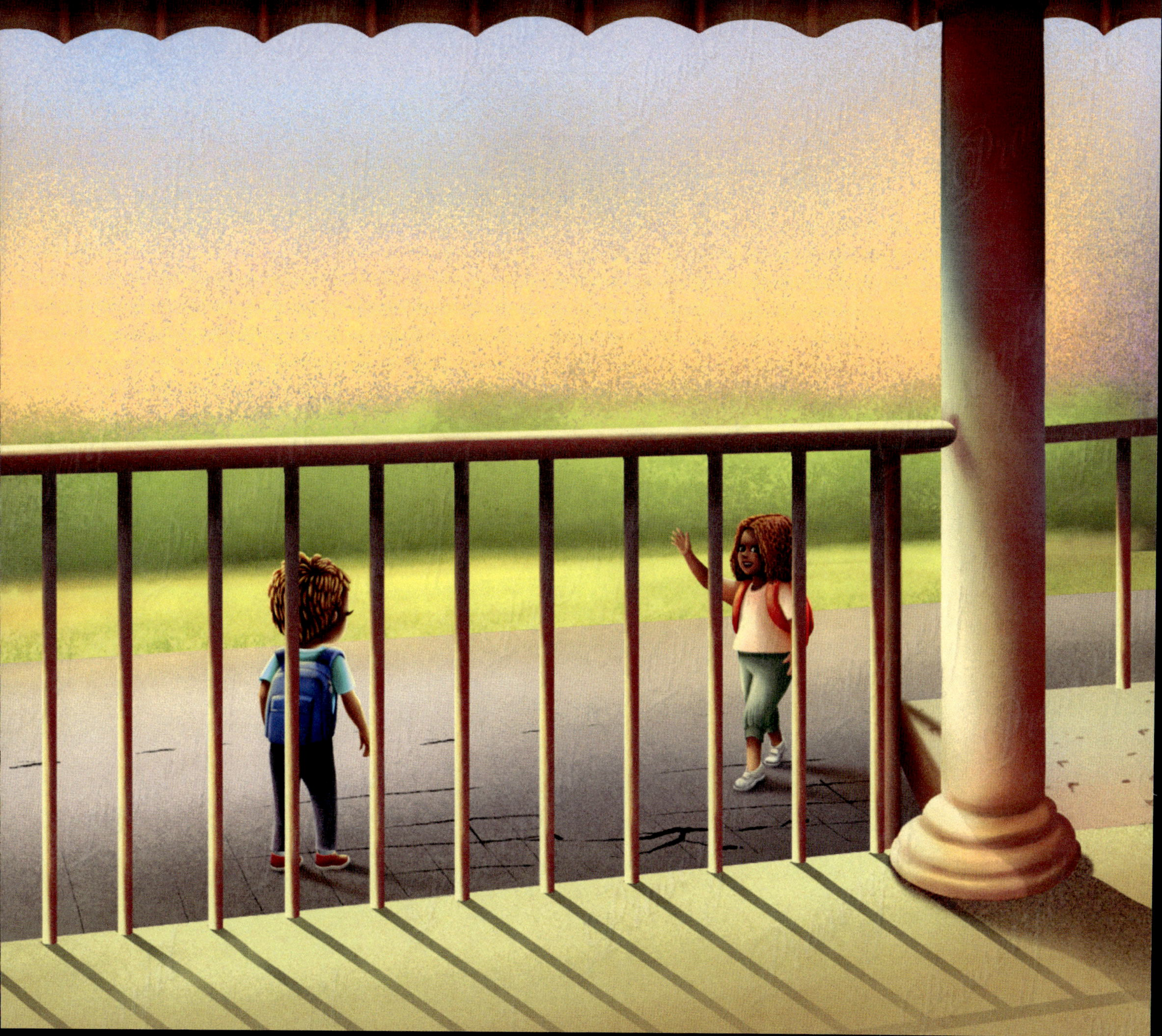

Moral of this story:

There is nothing cool or funny about being mean or judging a person. You don't know what someone may be going through. And being nice goes a long, long way!

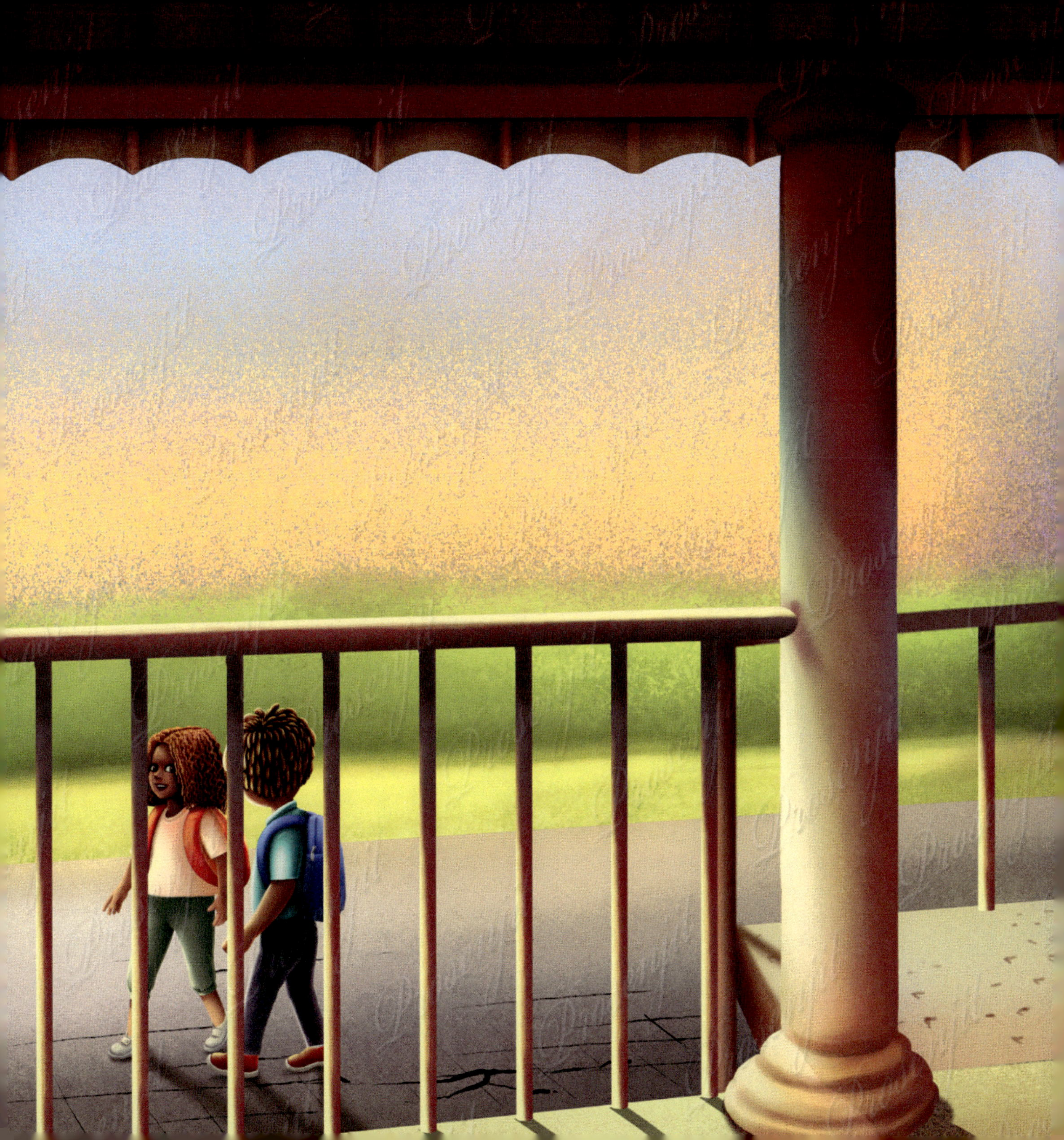

THE END

Made in the USA
Columbia, SC
08 July 2023